Elena's Birthday Surprise

Written by Liana Pérez *and* Patrice Samara
Illustrated by Carol Nicklaus *and* Susan Unger

TOYCHEST
interactive

Meet the Alphabet Kids: Allegra, Elena, Isaac, Oni, Umar, and Yang.

They call themselves the Alphabet Kids because that's where they
like to hang out — at the Alphabet Afterschool Center.
Every day they learn something new.

One special day, Elena came to the Alphabet Afterschool Center wearing a pretty party dress and a bow in her hair.

"*¡Buenos días!*" said Elena wishing her friends "Good day!" She had a big smile on her face. It was a very special day for Elena. It was her birthday.

The Alphabet Kids were all busy scurrying around the room.

"¡*Vamos!* Let's go!" Elena said to Allegra.

"Not now, Elena, I am drawing," said Allegra, barely looking up from her work.

Isaac was concentrating on building something tall with the blocks.

Oni was busy setting the table for their snack.

Umar and Yang were playing together in the toy corner.

So Elena took a book from the library shelf and started reading.
She was feeling sad because none of her friends had said
"Happy Birthday" to her all afternoon.

Mrs. Peters, their teacher, walked over to the reading corner.
"*Hola,*" Elena said quietly.
"What's wrong, Elena?" asked Mrs. Peters.

Elena said sadly, "Today is my birthday and nobody said 'Happy Birthday' to me."

"I'm sorry that you're sad, Elena. Why don't you come with me?" said Mrs. Peters with a big smile.

Mrs. Peters took Elena by the hand and they walked around the room together. Elena saw that everyone was still very busy.

Allegra had just finished her drawing and was picking up her crayons.

"I'm almost done with the blocks," said Isaac.

Umar and Yang said, "We're tidying up the toy corner."

"I am setting up for our snack," said Oni, placing little paper plates and napkins on the table.

"Let's go help Oni, now that we've finished putting our toys away," said Umar to Yang, walking to the snack table.

"Let's go over this way and see what's happening," Mrs. Peters said to Elena, with an even bigger smile.

Elena and Mrs. Peters slowly walked around the big wall of blocks that Isaac had built.

"Surprise!" shouted all the Alphabet Kids.
They hadn't forgotten Elena's birthday after all.

Umar and Yang had stacked up all the toys to greet Elena. Oni had decorated the table. There was even a birthday *piñata*! Allegra handed Elena the card she had made.

"You did it," said Mrs. Peters proudly to everyone. "You all worked together to give Elena a very happy birthday! *Feliz cumpleaños*, Elena."

"We made this party just for you, Elena!," they all cheered.

"*¡Fantástico!*" said Elena, as her friends all sang "Happy Birthday".

Elena blew out all the candles.

"Muchas gracias," Elena said, happily thanking everyone.
It was Elena's best birthday ever!